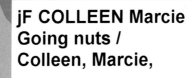

SUPER HAPPY PARTY BEARS

GOING NUTS

SUPER
HAPPY
PARTY
BEARS

GOING NUTS

MARCIE COLLEEN

[Imprint]
MAKE YOUR MARK

NEW YORK

 **[Imprint]** MAKE YOUR MARK

A part of Macmillan Children's Publishing Group,
a division of Macmillan Publishing Group, LLC

Super Happy Party Bears: Going Nuts

Library of Congress Cataloging-in-Publication Data is available.
ISBN 978-1-250-10049-8 (paperback) / ISBN 978-1-250-10050-4 (ebook)
Our books may be purchased in bulk for promotional, educational,
or business use. Please contact your local bookseller or the Macmillan
Corporate and Premium Sales Department at (800) 221-7945 ext. 5442
or by e-mail at MacmillanSpecialMarkets@macmillan.com.

Book design by Christine Kell
Imprint logo designed by Amanda Spielman
Illustrations by Steve James

First Edition—2017

1 3 5 7 9 10 8 6 4 2

mackids.com

If this isn't your book, keep your thieving paws off it.
Obey or may all your balloon animals look like bananas.

TO ALL THE TINY NUTS OUT THERE.
REMEMBER. THE TALLEST OAK IN THE
FOREST WAS ONCE JUST LIKE YOU.

CHAPTER ONE

Welcome to the Grumpy Woods!

Ha! That's impossible to say with a straight face.

Welcome to the Grump— ha-ha-ha! See?

No one is welcome in the Grumpy Woods.

So you may as well skedaddle before Sheriff Sherry hauls you off to City Hall. They don't like trespassers here.

The Grumpy Woods has seen its fair share of intruders, and every one of them has damaged the Woods in some way. First, the beavers came and chewed down all the trees to build their huge dam in the river. Second, a woodpecker pecked holes in everyone's homes and the Grumpy Wall. Third, a swarm of bees buzzed the townscritters and drowned their precious homes in honey. It's been disaster after disaster!

Now do you understand

why everyone here is GRUMPY?

Mayor Quill's list of rules, called

Mayoral Decrees to sound more

official, keeps getting longer and

longer. And his angry quill storms

have been coming with greater

frequency. He gets so mad when a

rule is broken that he shoots out quills everywhere. In fact, the Bee Incident left him with a really big bald spot.

The townscritters chipped in and created a special wig for the mayor to wear until new quills can grow in. Opal Owl donated

Mayor Quill

some of her feathers, Dawn Fawn

offered an old dust mop, and

Humphrey Hedgehog, the mayor's

own assistant deputy, collected

twigs and flowers. The wig was

quite large and very heavy, but

it covered the bald spot nicely.

However, Mayor Quill won't wear

it and instead hides in his office,

refusing to

be seen.

At a

recent

town hall meeting, the mayor spoke

from behind a curtain and said

again that something needed to be

done to keep outsiders *out.*

"We could try weaving a giant net to catch tressspassssserssss," suggested Sherry. "Like a web."

At the word *web*, Dawn Fawn grew exceptionally nervous and waved her duster wildly in the air.

"Cobwebs! Cobwebs! Icky sticky cobwebs!" she sang.

"We could booby-trap the entire perimeter," said Humphrey.

Squirrelly Sam poked his head under the curtain. "Maybe we should put up more curtains!

After all, they have kept everyone away from the mayor."

Mayor Quill quickly covered his bald spot with his paws and glared at Sam as the others dragged him back out by his bushy tail.

The townscritters don't agree on much, except one thing—they all agree they don't like the Super Happy Party Bears.

Why, you might ask?

Well, for one thing, the bears live at a cheery and welcoming place called the Party Patch, the Headquarters of Fun. Life is very different there. Life is super. Life is happy. And life is full of parties.

The townscritters don't do happy.

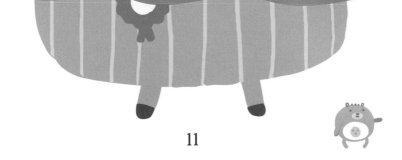

Instead, everyone in the Grumpy
Woods wakes up with their
knickers in a bunch and orders up
some breakfast—a piping-hot mug

of grouchy with an extra dash of *Get off my lawn!*

While the Super Happy Party Bears wake up BRIGHT-EYED AND BUSHY-TAILED to order up some breakfast—pancakes on a pogo stick, served with an extra dollop of WOO-HOO!

Nothing annoys the Grumpy Woods more.

Except when the bears have a party.

And they are always having a party.

2

CHAPTER TWO

The welcome-mat roof of the Party
Patch rattled as a wheelbarrow
rumbled through the door and
dumped a heap of assorted tree
nuts, mostly acorns, all over the
dance floor.

"That's the last load!" announced Jacks as he high-fived Stan the honeybee.

"Yay!" cheered the bears, who gathered eagerly around the nut pile.

Big Puff hit his drumsticks together. "ONE, TWO, THREE, FOUR!"

The Super Happy Party Band jammed out some crunching tunes as the rest of the bears stomped and clomped, crushing the nuts as they danced.

"This is the best doughnut-
making ever!" yelled the littlest
bear over the music.

"Simply smashing!" declared
Mops.

Once the nuts were sufficiently
trampled, they were sprinkled
on the iced doughnuts that lined

every surface
of the Party
Patch. The
doughnuts
were then

placed in pretty boxes, which were
tied with string.

These doughnuts were not for
the bears to eat. They were being
shipped all over the world through
Stan the honeybee's online Getsy
shop. Buyers were especially
crazy for these nutty honey-glazed
doughnuts—a special product

made only by the Super Happy

Party Bears.

"You still haven't told me where

you got all these nuts," buzzed Stan as he flipped through a tall stack of sales orders.

"We stumbled upon them," said Jacks.

Shades giggled. "Well, maybe not stumbled—more like danced."

During a particularly happy moment out in the Woods—as most moments are, for the Super Happy Party Bears—the bears began their Super Happy Party Dance. But when Shades slid to the right, he slipped on an acorn and kept on sliding right into a large rotten tree stump. Out tumbled the biggest stash of nuts this side of the Grumpy River!

"Well, my customers are loving these Nuts About Honey

doughnuts," said Stan. "Sales have
been through the roof! You bears
put the *dough* in doughnuts.
Ka-ching, ka-ching!"

"NUT-TASTIC!"

cheered the bears.

They had just finished boxing up the last batch when there was a knock on the Party Patch door. The bears sent the shipment off with Stan's delivery bees and hurried over to the door to welcome their visitor.

"ONE! TWO! THREE! WHO CAN IT BEEEEEEEEEEE?" sang

the bears before swinging the door open wide.

Three squirrels stood on the stoop—Squirrelly Sam and two others. They looked extremely grumpy.

"SQUIRRELS!!!" the bears cheered.

The squirrels just glared at them.

Squirrelly Sam adjusted his glasses and cleared his throat. "You didn't hear this from me, but you bears are in BIG trouble with the Twitchy Tails."

"The Twitchy Tails? How cute!" said Jigs, and she gave her maracas a shake while all the other bears twitched their tails. "Who are the Twitchy Tails?"

"We are! And there is nothing—" started one squirrel.

"—cute about the Twitchy Tails," finished the other.

Filbert and Hazel were twin squirrels. Alike in every way except appearance. It was often said that the brother and sister shared a brain. (And squirrel brains are known to be tiny.)

"Let me put this nicely,"

continued Sam. "GIVE US OUR
NUTS BACK, YOU THIEVES!"

"You mean the nuts on the
doughnuts we just shipped off to
Honolulu?" asked Mops.

"Hono—?" said Filbert.

"—lulu?" said Hazel.

"Yeah. Hepcats from all over are digging our Nuts About Honey doughnuts," said Big Puff.

"Are you saying our nuts are—
are—are gone?" Sam's eyes grew
crazy. His tail started to twitch.

The three squirrels panicked and
ran around in circles.

"We're going to—"

"—STARVE!"

"I feel—"

"—FAINT!"

"FEAR MY SQUIRRELLY WRATH!" threatened Sam.

"Now, wait a minute," said Jacks. "No one is going to starve. There are plenty more nuts in the Grumpy Woods."

The trio froze and looked at Jacks suspiciously.

"Come on. We'll show you.

Follow us," said the bears.

CHAPTER THREE

The bears marched like a
cheerful parade through the
Grumpy Woods. The squirrels
scurried along in and out of line,
sometimes even climbing up the
legs and arms of the bears to ask
repeatedly, "Are we there yet?"

"Did you hear that?" asked Hazel.

"It was my stomach growling," said Filbert.

"No. It was *my* stomach growling," said Hazel.

"No. It was mine. I'm famished," said Filbert.

"I'm more famished," said Hazel.

The sibling bickering continued as the bears trooped deeper and deeper into the Woods. Sam anxiously sat atop Jacks's head. But he moved around so much he

kept pushing Jacks's headband

down over his eyes.

"Is that it?" Sam asked every few seconds, desperate to find the nuts they were promised.

Finally, they stopped in front of a tangle of brush and shrubs.

"Here we are," sang the bears, beaming with pride.

"What? Here?" a jittery Sam said. "These aren't nut-bearing trees. There are no nuts here! WE ARE DOOMED!"

The three squirrels panicked once again and ran in circles until their noses met up with their tails.

"Silly squirrels!" said the littlest

bear. "It's a tunnel." The bears
pulled back the shrubs to uncover
a long, dark passageway.

"See?" said the bears.

The Twitchy Tails peered down
the tunnel and grew twitchier.

"Is this a trick?" asked Sam,
turning his head so he was looking
at the bears with one eye only.

"No!" The bears giggled. "It's nuts!"

"I'll lead the way," volunteered Flips, who somehow turned his party hat into a flashlight.

One after another, the bears and their squirrel friends entered the burrow. The dirt walls were

scribbled with signs of warning and cartoons of fierce-looking chipmunks.

"'Turn around!' 'Paws off!' 'Go back!'" read Shades, who had to push his star-shaped glasses atop his head for the dark journey. "What do you think these mean?"

"They are hieroglyphs," explained Bubs as he blew bubbles. "Obviously a long-ago civilization's communications describing their ancient dance moves."

The bears oohed and instantly turned the burrow into a disco.

Turn 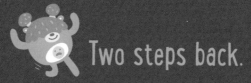 around.

Two steps back.

Clap. Clap.  Yay!

But Sam scuttled up Jigs and stood tall on the bear's head to interrupt the ancient dance party.

"WHAT ABOUT THE NUTS?"

"Easy does it, Bushy Tail," said Big Puff, shining Flips's flashlight to reveal the largest heap of nuts any squirrel had ever seen.

The three squirrels froze and turned their heads so they were looking at the stockpile with only one eye each. Their eyes grew bulgier. They stood perfectly still, as if the pile would disappear if they moved.

"Go on," said the littlest bear. "Take all you want!"

So they did. They stuffed their squirrelly cheek pouches like grocery bags. When they couldn't squeeze in any more nuts, they darted off and returned with empty cheeks to fill again. And again. And

again. Until all that was left was a bare dirt floor in an echoing tunnel.

The Twitchy Tails were happy. The Super Happy Party Bears were happy. All was well.

"Yay! We love happy endings!" cheered the bears, and they turned to journey back to the Party Patch. But not before one last ancient dance.

Turn  around.

Two steps  back.

 Clap. Clap. Yay!

CHAPTER FOUR

The Super Happy Party Bears
returned to the Party Patch all set
to party the day away, but they
were quickly interrupted by a
knock on the door.

Knock, knock, knock.

"ONE! TWO! THREE! WHO CAN

IT BEEEEEEEEEEEE?" sang the
bears before swinging the door
open wide.

Two chipmunks in police
uniforms stood on the stoop. They
looked extremely serious.

"CHIPMUNKS!!!" the bears
cheered.

One chipmunk took off his
sunglasses to get a better look at
the bears.

"I'm Officer Jon. This is my
partner, Officer Pouch."

Pouch gave a slight nod, and
his overly large cheek pouches
nodded, too.

"May we come in?" asked Officer
Jon.

"Yay! We love company!" cheered the bears. They yanked the officers into the Party Patch and put a cup of juice in their paws.

"We're actually here on very important official business. We're with CHiPs—Chipmunk Hijinks

Patrol. We are investigating some stolen nuts. Any of this sound familiar?" asked Officer Jon.

"This is the most special morning ever!" cheered the bears.

"I can see myself in your sunglasses," said Little Puff.

Pouch and Jon were not amused. They set their juice cups down and surveyed the crowd.

"Mind if we ask you a few questions?" asked Officer Jon. Officer Pouch pulled a very slobbery notebook and pen out of his oversized cheeks and handed them to Officer Jon.

While Officer Jon prepared to interrogate the bears, Officer Pouch looked for clues around the Party Patch. Anything

that appeared to be evidence,

including a few stray doughnuts,

was squirrelled away in Pouch's pouches for investigation later.

Officer Jon glanced down at the dust-covered bear paws. He held up an acorn. "Does this look familiar?"

"Oh no," said Jacks. "The Twitchy Tails must have dropped it when they were taking all those nuts out of that tunnel."

Pouch and Jon shared a look
and nodded their heads. Pouch's
cheeks jiggled.

"Thank you so much for finding
it, Officer," said Mops. "We will
return it to them right away."

"We have a better idea," said

Officer Jon. "Why don't we go with you? To, ah, make sure justice is served."

"Yay! Let's go be good neighbors!" cheered the bears.

Officer Jon put his sunglasses back on and stuffed the notebook and pen into Officer Pouch's cheeks.

"The Twitchy Tails will be surprised!" said Jacks, excited to see his new friends again.

Officer Jon smirked. "Very surprised."

CHAPTER FIVE

The Super Happy Party Bears led Pouch and Jon through undergrowth and overgrowth until they reached the hidden thicket of the Twitchy Tails' clubhouse.

Jacks ran ahead of the rest and was just about to knock on the

door when
Officer Pouch
stepped in front of
him.

"We're going to
go about this quiet-
like," said Officer Jon.

"You mean like a surprise party?" asked the littlest bear.

"Exactly," said Officer Jon. "A super-stealthy surprise party."

The officers peeked through the window. They could see the Twitchy Tails—Sam, Filbert, and

Hazel—gathered around a stack of
maps. Twitching.

"All right, everyone, hide in the
bushes. Officer Pouch and I will
let you know when to come out,"
ordered Officer Jon.

"And yell 'SURPRISE'?" asked
Jacks.

"Yes," answered Officer Jon,
rolling his eyes.

Officer Pouch retrieved a roll
of yellow DO NOT CROSS tape from
his cheeks and began unrolling it,
with the bears behind it. But before
he could finish, three chipmunks

popped out from the bushes. The Puffy Cheeks—Coco, Macadamia, and Nutmeg—were the most ruthless group of chipmunks in the Grumpy Woods. They prided themselves on having the most exclusive collection of nuts.

"What's taking so long?" they demanded in unison.

"I'm starving," whined Nutmeg.

"I'm so hungry that I'm hallucinating," said Macadamia. "I'm seeing rainbow-colored bears!"

"Step aside, everyone," said Coco. "This Puffy Cheek is taking matters into her own hands." And with a powerful kick, Coco burst through the door of the Twitchy Tails' hideout.

"SURPRISE!" yelled the bears.

"Freeze!" ordered Officer Jon. Sam, Filbert, and Hazel were already frozen, because that is what squirrels do. The bears joined in and froze, too.

Officer Pouch searched the clubhouse, using a flashlight and a magnifying glass. Both had been pulled from his cheeks and were a little slobbery.

"Where's the goods?" asked Coco.

"Wh-wh-what goods?" asked Sam.

"The goods you stole from *our* nuthouse!" she continued.

Pouch and Jon riffled through the maps. They were maps of the Grumpy Woods, and each was labeled ONE-TAIL WILLY'S NUT TREASURE. But instead of Xs marking any spots, the maps were covered in question marks.

"What are these?" asked Officer Jon. "Will they tell us where the stash is?"

"Your stash is in my belly," said Sam, smugly patting his satisfied tummy.

Macadamia and Nutmeg groaned as their own bellies rumbled.

"Then give us your haul for winter!" demanded Coco.

"They stole it for their doughnuts!" Sam pointed at the Super Happy Party Bears.

"Are there any more nuts left in the Grumpy Woods?" asked Nutmeg.

"Now, that's the million-dollar question," came a voice from a dark corner of the clubhouse. Out limped Ace, a retired flying squirrel who made his home with the Twitchy Tails.

"Squirrels always know—" said Filbert.

"—where nuts are buried," finished Hazel. Ace just laughed. "That's what One-Tail Willy used to say. But to this day, no one can find his legendary stash. We've been digging up these woods for years."

"Wait a minute. His name was One-Tail Willy? Don't all squirrels have only one tail?" asked Macadamia.

"That's not the point," said
Ace. "The point is, if we could just
locate One-Tail Willy's treasure,
there would be enough for all
of us."

"What are you trying to say?"
asked Coco.

The Twitchy Tails
and the Puffy
Cheeks lost
control.

"WE'RE GOING TO STARVE!!!" It was one thing they could agree on.

CHAPTER SIX

War was declared in the Grumpy Woods. A war of nuts. A war fighting over nuts, to be exact.

At their clubhouse, the Puffy Cheeks were planning their first move.

"By my calculations, we have

73

several months before new nuts can be harvested here in the Grumpy Woods. Therefore, One-Tail Willy's legendary stash is our only hope of survival. We need a strategy to outwit those dimwits and find the treasure first," said Coco. "What are squirrels scared of?"

"Bacon?" guessed Macadamia.

"Cake?" guessed Nutmeg.

"Can we go search for cake and bacon to scare those Twitchy Tails with?" the two begged as their tummies groaned with hunger.

"Stop thinking with your stomachs!" said Coco. "Focus that hunger to defeat the enemy."

"I could focus better with cake," mumbled Nutmeg.

Officer Pouch pulled a *How to Get Rid of Pesky Squirrels* book out of his sagging cheeks.

Officer Jon skimmed through

the fairly large volume and came to a conclusion. "It says here that squirrels are scared of everything. Including other squirrels."

"Precisely what I thought," said Coco. "Here's our plan. We place mirrors all over the Grumpy Woods. Those silly squirrels will see their reflections, freak out, and scare themselves right out of the Woods for good. We won't even have to break a sweat chasing them. Once they're gone, One-Tail Willy's haul is all ours."

The Puffy Cheeks broke into a fit of evil laughter and then got to work setting up the mirrors. And it worked . . . kind of.

Hazel and Filbert were on duty, searching for the lost One-Tail Willy stash, when they came upon one of the mirrors. They both froze.

"Don't—" said Hazel.

"—move," finished Filbert.

"They are both looking—" started Hazel.

"—right at me," finished Filbert.

"Actually, at me," said Hazel.

"Well, the mangy one is looking at me," said Filbert.

The standoff lasted until . . .

SPLAT!

Opal Owl, not seeing the mirror, flew straight into it. Her beak bent out of shape. It didn't take long for her to track down where the mirrors had come from. Let's just say that the last thing a chipmunk should do is anger an owl.

Seeing the Puffy Cheeks chased by Opal gave the Twitchy Tails a brilliant idea. They set up fake owl decoys all over the Woods. The chipmunks were terrified! Opal Owl seemed to be everywhere! It wasn't until they saw Dawn Fawn dusting

the heads of the owls that the
chipmunks realized they had been
tricked.

The Puffy Cheeks retaliated by
sprinkling cayenne pepper and

peppermint far and wide. But the clouds of spice got into *every* townscritter's nose, causing a sneeze-a-thon of epic proportions. Mayor Quill's nose got a tickle so bad that he sneezed thirteen times in a row.

"Achooo!"

"Gesundheit, sir," said Humphrey.

"Achooo!"

"Gesundheit, sir."

"Achooo!"

"Gesundheit, sir."

Mayor Quill stomped his foot. He shook from head to toe. Just before

the mayor exploded, Humphrey

rolled into a defensive ball.

Achoooooooo ka-boom!

Mayoral Decree 1,973 was

declared: "'Gesundheit' shall only

be said after the *first* sneeze."

Sam suddenly appeared, scrambling from the branches above to hang his head upside down in the doorway.

"You didn't hear this from me, but apparently chipmunks are repelled by, um, fox urine," he whispered. "But I can't find a fox

anywhere in the Grumpy Woods. Is this a bad time to ask if you would pee in this cup?" Sam held out a cup. Humphrey covered his eyes in embarrassment, and the mayor . . .

KA-BOOM!

Quills exploded everywhere. Again.

The Twitchy Tails needed another strategy. That's when Ace unveiled the motion-activated Chipmunkinator, a primitive contraption made of tree bark and some long, braided grasses, that launched water balloons. Problem was, the Chipmunkinator did not know the difference between the movement of a chipmunk or a snake or a rabbit or even a mayor.

Mayor Quill, taking a break from the grueling work that comes with

being a mayor, was sunbathing on
the private, members-only official
City Hall patio. Of course, he was
the only member, and he liked
it that way. Humphrey was only
allowed on the patio to fan the
mayor with a large leaf when he got
overheated. Without warning there
was a—

SPLOOOOOOOOSH!

The Chipmunkinator soaked
them both.

"That's it!" yelled Quill.
Humphrey shielded himself with
the large leaf fan just in case.

CHAPTER SEVEN

Mayor Quill demanded an
emergency town meeting and
insisted that *everyone* attend.

Still dripping wet, Quill stood in
a puddle behind his podium. He
banged his gavel several times,
sending water droplets through

the air. There was no calming the Puffy Cheeks and the Twitchy Tails. Of course, Officer Jon and Officer Pouch tried to keep the peace, but once they remembered that they, too, were chipmunks and that they didn't have any nuts, they joined the panic.

The squabbling boomed through the Grumpy Woods, and soon the other townscritters were caught up in the commotion.

"By order of Mayoral Decree number one thousand nine hundred and seventy-four, the Twitchy Tails and the Puffy Cheeks must share everything equally," Mayor Quill proclaimed.

Mayoral Decree

1,974

The Twitchy Tails and the Puffy Cheeks must share everything equally.

Mayor Quill

"Yay! We love sharing!" cheered the bears.

"But—" started Sam.

"You heard the mayor," said Humphrey Hedgehog. "Absolutely everything."

"Using this can of paint and this paintbrush," explained Mayor

Quill, "Humphrey will oversee the operation and make sure that everything within the Woods is divided in half. One half for the Puffy Cheeks and one half for the Twitchy Tails."

To demonstrate, Humphrey took the paint and paintbrush and, with an authoritative flourish, drew a line straight down the room. He

accidentally painted right over the
paw of the littlest bear, who giggled
and said, "Sharing tickles!"

Once the Puffy Cheeks and
the Twitchy Tails were standing
on opposite sides of the line,
Quill banged his gavel to end the
meeting.

Humphrey took his job very seriously. Soon a line was drawn down a tree through the Woods. Over every rock. Even Sheriff Sherry.

"Justice must be equally distributed," said Coco.

"We get the end with the hat," said Sam.

However, it wasn't always so easy to determine sides.

While the Puffy Cheeks were busy digging up one side of the woods, looking for the lost treasure, the Twitchy Tails were digging on the other side. They frantically dug and dug, zigging and zagging this way and that way, creating tunnels. Tunnels that led the Puffy Cheeks to pop up on the

Twitchy side, while the Twitchy

Tails popped up on the Puffy side.

"Get out of our territory!"

demanded Coco.

"You get out of *our* territory,"

demanded Sam.

"We'll tell Sheriff Sherry on you,"

said Nutmeg.

"Your end of Sherry can't hear,"

taunted Hazel and Filbert.

Just then the littlest bear came

skipping down the painted line. "Hi, friends," he greeted the chipmunks and the squirrels.

The Puffy Cheeks grabbed the littlest bear's arm and pulled. "You are our friend!"

"I am!" cheered the littlest bear.

The Twitchy Tails grabbed the

littlest bear's other arm and pulled back. "He's our friend!"

The littlest bear giggled. "We're dancing!"

The littlest bear was pulled back and forth. Back and forth. The two sides locked eyes. And then . . .

"WE DECLARE A RUMBLE!" they all yelled. It was yet another thing they could agree on.

CHAPTER EIGHT

Both the Twitchy Tails and the
Puffy Cheeks prepared for an
ultimate showdown—the Rumble,
as it was called. The Rumble would
settle the battle between the two
sides once and for all. It was to be
at high noon (which is the same as

noon, but with an extra word) on the Grumpy Grassland.

"What's a rumble?" the littlest bear asked Bubs.

"It's a dance-off in which opposing teams dance until a winner is declared," Bubs explained.

"Ooh," said the bears.

"What a delightful way to settle disagreements," said Shades. "Let's see if either side needs our help."

The Super Happy Party Bears boogied straight to the underground clubhouse of the Puffy Cheeks. One by one, the bears shimmied down a very tight tunnel and popped out in a

cavernous room deep beneath the Woods. At the far end was a door. Officer Jon and Officer Pouch were standing guard.

"I think you have all done quite enough," said Officer Jon.

"But we are here to help with the Rumble," explained Shades. "We have some moves we think

will come in handy for the Puffy

Cheeks."

"What kind of moves?" asked

Officer Jon.

"Moves that really pack a

punch," said Jacks.

"Now you're talking," said Officer

Jon.

The officers stepped aside and let the bears into the clubhouse, where an assembly line was in progress. Coco was bent over some blueprints, barking orders at Macadamia and Nutmeg, who were whittling twigs with their teeth.

"Gnaw faster!" yelled Coco.

"But I'm so weak," said Nutmeg.

"I haven't eaten a nut for an entire DAY!"

"And I'm even weaker," added Macadamia.

The bears jumped into action.

"IT'S SUPER HAPPY RUMBLE TIME! SUPER HAPPY RUMBLE TIME!"

Slide to  the right.

Hop  to the left.

Shimmy, shimmy, shake.

 Strike a pose.

"We're here to help," said the littlest bear.

"Fine," said Coco, unamused. "We need five of these catapults."

"Ooh! We love arts and crafts!" said the bears.

The bears got to work and finished the catapults in record time. Then they covered the catapults with sparkles and rainbow paint. They even decorated the boulders with fun messages like WE LOVE RUMBLES and

ROCK ON. Finally, they showed their handiwork to the chipmunks.

"Not quite the fierce message we wanted to send," mumbled Officer Jon.

"Are these going to be used to launch glitter into the sky while

we do our Rumble dance?" asked
Mops.

"Something like that," said
Coco. "Now help me with these
boulders."

CHAPTER NINE

The Puffy Cheeks said they were all ready for the Rumble. And although the Super Happy Party Bears wished they had practiced the dance together, they could understand not wanting to share their smooth moves until high noon.

"Maybe the Twitchy Tails need some extra preparation help, too," said the littlest bear. So the bears trekked to the Twitchy Tails' clubhouse.

Sam greeted them at the door. He was wearing oversized wings made out of a few of Opal's feathers (they'd fallen out when she smacked into the mirror) and some large leaves sewn together like a quilt.

"Oooh. We love costumes!" cheered the bears.

The bears joined the rest of the

Twitchy Tails, who were also wearing wings. They were seated on the floor, listening to Ace, who was pointing at a large map on the wall.

"So the pinecone airstrike will depart from this tree to the east," continued the flying squirrel.

Hazel raised her hand. "Why do we have to fly?"

"We're not flying squirrels," said Filbert.

"We've been through this," explained Sam. "Ace cannot lead the mission. His blood sugar is way too low to fly at such altitudes. We all need to do our part to seize control of the nut reserves in the Grumpy Woods."

"Our blood sugar is low, too!" whined Hazel.

"Yeah. I'm so dizzy!" whimpered Filbert.

"What about the bears?" asked Ace.

All eyes turned to the Super Happy Party Bears.

"What did you guys eat for breakfast?" asked Sam.

"Doughnuts!" cheered the bears.

"And mid-morning snack?"

"Doughnuts!" said the bears.

"No low blood sugar here," said
Sam. "Welcome to the Twitchy
Tails!"

"We need to get the bears to the
pine trees before high noon. Follow
me and look sharp," said Ace.

"Do we get costumes, too?"
asked the littlest bear.

The Twitchy Tails crawled on
their bellies, careful not to be seen
so close to the Grumpy Grassland

before high noon. The bears, of course, thought this was all part of the dance.

"I love crawling," said Jacks.

"Maybe we should add a roll or two," suggested Shades.

"And a spin," added Mops.

The Twitchy Tails hushed them and kept crawling, stopping at the

base of a ginormous pine tree. Its
top was hidden in the clouds.

"We need you to climb to the
top of this tree, gathering as many
pinecones as you can on your way
up," said Sam.

"We love climbing trees!"
cheered the bears.

"Where are our costumes?"
asked the littlest bear again.

"When you get to the top,
wait quietly until you hear the
code word, and then chuck the

pinecones toward the Grumpy Grassland," instructed Ace.

"What's the code word?" asked Jacks.

"Rumble," answered Sam matter-of-factly. And with that, the Twitchy Tails scurried off to ready themselves, and the bears started their long climb upward. It was nearly high noon.

CHAPTER TEN

It was high noon (which, again, is the same as noon, but with an extra word), and all was peaceful on the Grumpy Grassland until the squeaky wheels of five technicolored catapults rolled in

from the west.

The Puffy Cheeks were ready.

From the east, three winged
squirrels and a limping flying
squirrel emerged. The Twitchy
Tails were ready.

Above, the pine tree seemed to

giggle with anticipation. The Super Happy Party Bears were ready.

As the two opposing sides faced off, there came a commotion from the south. It was the townscritters marching to stop the Rumble.

"By order of Mayoral Decree

one thousand nine hundred and

seventy-five, there is to be no

Rumble!" hollered Mayor Quill

loudly enough to be heard by all,

including the Super Happy Party

Bears, who were waiting for just

such a code word.

At the word *Rumble*, hundreds of pinecones rained from the branches above, along with a dozen bears who were ready to finally show their Rumble dance moves. The bears landed in the center of the three groups and struck a pose.

"Hit it," cued Big Puff as Tunes pressed PLAY on her boom box.

The bears popped to the left. They stomped to the right. Roll, roll, robot arms.

The music was catchy. The townscritters, the Twitchy Tails, and the Puffy Cheeks looked on, dismayed. Sam started to tap his toes.

The bears continued dancing. They wriggled across the grass like worms, spun on their heads, and then balanced on one paw as they bounced in circles.

"SUPER HAPPY RUMBLE TIME!
SUPER HAPPY RUMBLE TIME!"

The ground was quaking and
shaking as the bears encouraged
everyone to stomp to the rhythm.
It was difficult to resist. The Puffy
Cheeks stomped. The Twitchy Tails
clomped.

"Stop rumbling this instant!" yelled Mayor Quill.

"Are they dancing or fighting?" asked Humphrey.

Stomp. Stomp. Hop-hop. Clompy-clomp.

Just then the ground shuddered. It rumbled. And as the littlest bear stamped his littlest paw, the field caved in. Down tumbled the Super Happy Party Bears, the Twitchy Tails, the Puffy Cheeks, and the townscritters.

"Aw, nuts," said Coco as she noticed the five destroyed catapults sticking out of the rubble.

"Exactly!" said Sam. "NUTS!"

Everyone was buried in an enormous load of nuts.

"It's One-Tail Willy's stash," said Ace. "The Super Happy Party Bears found it!"

"They saved the day!" cheered the Twitchy Tails and the Puffy Cheeks.

"Looks like it's time for a Harvest Nut-Gathering Party!" cheered the bears. "We'll make the doughnuts!"

Humphrey, still taking his painting duty seriously, helped distribute the hoard with the rest of the townscritters.

132

"One for the Puffy Cheeks. One for the Twitchy Tails," he said, making two very large piles.

The chipmunks stuffed their cheeks while Hazel and Filbert hurried off to hide their stash in a *new* secret spot. A spot that wouldn't be danced into by the Super Happy Party Bears.

Soon One-Tail Willy's treasure was equally divided.

One last nut remained. Coco reached for it. Sam reached for it. Coco pulled one way. Sam pulled the other way. Everyone held their breath, unsure of what would

happen. The chipmunk and the squirrel locked eyes. And then . . . together they handed the nut to the Super Happy Party Bears.

"Thank you for saving us all," said Sam.

"Use this for your next batch of doughnuts," added Coco.

The bears cheered.

And you know what? The townscritters cheered, too. They were feeling *a little less grumpy*.

THE END.

ABOUT THE AUTHOR

In previous chapters, Marcie Colleen
has been a teacher, an actress, and
a nanny, but now she spends her
days writing children's books! She
lives in her very own Party Patch,
Headquarters of Fun, with her husband
and their mischievous sock monkey
in San Diego, California. Occasionally,
there are even doughnuts. This is her
first chapter book series.

Don't Miss the Other SUPER HAPPY PARTY BEARS Books

SUPER HAPPY PARTY BEARS

GNAWING AROUND

MARCIE COLLEEN

SUPER HAPPY PARTY BEARS

KNOCK KNOCK on WOOD

MARCIE COLLEEN

SUPER HAPPY PARTY BEARS

STAYING A HIVE

MARCIE COLLEEN

SUPER HAPPY PARTY BEARS

GOING NUTS

MARCIE COLLEEN